ANIMAL TALES FROM INDIA

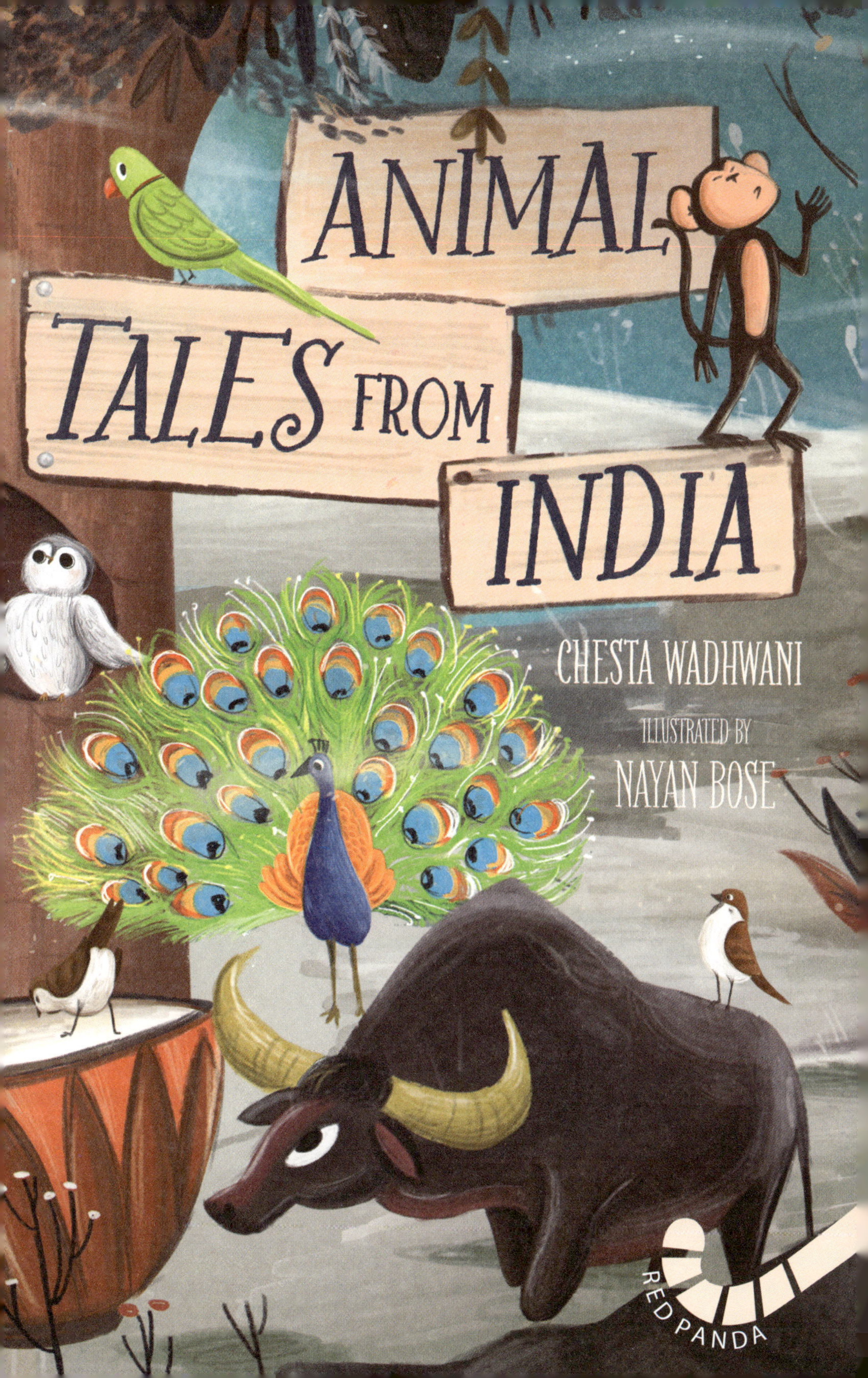
ANIMAL
TALES FROM
INDIA
CHESTA WADHWANI
ILLUSTRATED BY
NAYAN BOSE
RED PANDA

For my mom, Devika,
my first light in the universe.

Published by Red Panda, an imprint of Westland Books, a division of Nasadiya Technologies Private Limited, in 2025

No. 269/2B, First Floor, 'Irai Arul', Vimalraj Street, Nethaji Nagar, Alapakkam Main Road, Maduravoyal, Chennai 600095

ISBN: 9789360454937

10 9 8 7 6 5 4 3 2 1

Book design by Pratik M. Kalekar

This is a work of fiction. Names, characters, organisations, places, events and incidents are either products of the author's imagination or used fictitiously.

Printed at Parksons Graphics Pvt. Ltd

Welcome to *Animal Tales from India*—a magical journey into forests, riversides and village fields where cunning jackals, clever rabbits, vain owls and brave little birds live out tales that are as timeless as they are wise.

Inspired by Indian folktales and ancient storytelling traditions, each story in this book is more than just a fun adventure. At their heart, these tales carry quiet lessons—about courage, friendship, honesty, pride and the power of kindness. A rabbit outwits a lion not with strength but with cleverness. A tiny fish teaches a greedy fisherman a lesson he won't forget. A parrot dares to take on a blazing forest fire. These are not just animal stories—they are stories of spirit.

So, turn the page. A forest full of characters awaits you. And who knows? You might just find a little bit of yourself in them.

CONTENTS

1. THE CLEVER FISH AND THE GREEDY FISHERMAN

Long ago, there lived a fisherman in a quaint village by a sparkling river. The village, lined with trees and green canopies, was home to many animals. Every morning, under the sun, the fisherman would walk to the riverbank, where he would throw his net into the deep, blue river to catch his lot for the day. The river had fish of all colours and sizes. He would take his fresh catch to the market in the town nearby and sell it for money.

One day, while fishing for a catch, he had an unusual encounter. He waited patiently for the fish to make their way into his net for a long time. But the fish just didn't show up. 'Maybe it is a fish holiday,' he grumbled. He decided to move to a better spot.

He pulled the net out and moved under the shade of a huge tree whose branches snaked over the water, covering the sun. After a few minutes, he threw his net into the river. This time the net twitched almost immediately. The fisherman bent down to have a closer look; a tiny fish was struggling in the net. The fisherman was disappointed by the size of the fish.

The fish noticed his sad face and thought of a way to save her life. It pleaded, 'Dear kind fisherman, please let go of me.' The fisherman did not pay the fish any attention and continued to draw his net out of the water.

The fish tried a different tone. 'Hey fisherman bhaiya, I know you were looking for a raja machhli but you found me instead. I am a small freshwater fish—a mourola machh. Let me go. I'll make it worth your while!'

This time, the fisherman listened. The little fish continued. 'If you let me go, I'll bring my friends here tomorrow. You'll have a net full of fish! Just think of the fishy feast you can sell!'

The fisherman's eyes widened at the thought of catching many fish. He thought, 'If I allow this little fish to go, then I can get many fish tomorrow without much effort. And I will make good money!' Before the smart, tiny fish could repeat the question, the fisherman nodded and said, 'Yes, I will let you go but don't forget your promise. I will wait for you and your friends.'

The little fish was overjoyed. She had saved herself! 'Hurray! I am going back home,' she laughed.

The fisherman released the little fish into the water. The fish swam away happily.

The next day, the fisherman reached the riverbank. He couldn't control his excitement. He couldn't wait for a large catch and the money he would get selling it. He was inching closer to his dream of being rich.

Once he reached the spot, he looked for the tiny fish. But there was no one. He waited and waited but found nothing—neither the fish nor her friends. Soon the fisherman realised that he had been outsmarted by the little fish. 'The little fish played me like a fiddle,' he cried.

His face dropped. He returned home without any catch, neither big nor small. 'Well, that's the last time I fell for a fish's tricks!' he said sheepishly, trying to make light of his misfortune.

2. THE MUSICAL DONKEY

In a mountainous village lined with flowerbeds and leafy peepal trees, there lived a washerman and his donkey. They had a simple ritual: every day as the sun emerged from behind the rocky mountains, the donkey would carry the washerman's bags. In the evening, the washerman would set the donkey free in a nearby field to feast on grass. The donkey, however, was bored of this ritual that ended every day with plain grass. He was looking for an exciting turn of events. 'I want some fresh, juicy food—grapes, perhaps vegetables! Ooh la la,' he sang to himself. The donkey loved music and singing but did not have a talent for it.

One day, when the washerman had retired for the day, the donkey sneaked into a nearby farm full of ripe vegetables. He ate to his heart's content. Now the donkey looked forward to the nights—as soon as the washerman started snoring on his bed, the donkey quietly entered the farm and picked out the vegetables of his choice.

One day while wandering around the farm he met a jackal. They became friends instantly. Every night they ventured into the farm and had a good time talking and munching on vegetables; by dawn, the donkey would be back home to the washerman, ready to carry the bags. This routine went on for many days. One day, the jackal told the donkey. 'Sir, this morning I stumbled upon a new field—not too far from here.

And there I ate the yummiest of cucumbers. So ripe, so fresh—it's a real buffet.'

The donkey's mouth watered at the mention of cucumbers. 'Let's go tonight,' the donkey said to his friend.

The jackal laughed. 'I am sure I will find plenty of small animals, and my tummy will thank me for it.'

So that night they walked through the village, crossed a small forest and found themselves on a farm with the best cucumbers. The donkey, his belly full, sat down and gazed at the moon. It was a full moon. 'My friend, thank you for bringing me here. I feel so happy tonight—it makes me want to sing to this gorgeous moon.'

The jackal immediately said, 'Please don't. We are stealing from this field. Your voice will wake the farmers and we'll be caught and how!'

The donkey did not like his friend's fearful response. He sang anyway. 'You are a wild animal, you have no clue how music can move us,' the donkey told the jackal.

The jackal was smart, so he made a plan. 'Sir, of course, you must sing! Please wait for me to leave this field so that I can keep an eye on the farmers.' The jackal ran like there was no tomorrow and hid outside the field.

The donkey looked up to the moon and began to bray at the top of his not-so-melodious voice. The farmers woke up when they heard the noise.

In the light of the full moon, the farmers chased the singing donkey out of the field. They pelted sticks and even stones at the donkey. The donkey stopped braying and limped his way back home, crying a little. 'No more cucumbers!' he wept.

The jackal emerged from his hiding place laughing. 'Great singing! You have been rewarded well—I see that.'

3. THE FOOLISH LION AND THE CLEVER RABBIT

In a forest far away, there lived a lion who would roar for his meals from his den, sending the animals in a panic-stricken scurry. The lion would roar: 'Raaaaaaa!' trampling the grass and twigs in the thick, green forest. He would hunt and kill goats, sheep, cows and rabbits even when he was not hungry. The forest animals feared that soon no one would live to see another day.

So the animals decided to offer one amongst them to the lion every day. They went into the lion's den and called out to him. 'Your Majesty! We have a request. Please hear us out.' The lion roared, salivating at the sight of the animals.

'What do you want? You all are making me hungry!'

'Your Majesty, we beg you to please stop killing us like this. Please stay in your den, Sir. Why waste your energy to go hunt for a meal? We will send you one animal to eat every day, so you won't have to hunt for your meals ever again.

The lion agreed. From that day onwards, one animal went to the den as the lion's meal.

One day, it was the rabbit's turn to be the lion's dinner. The rabbit peered into the den with his ruby-red eyes and thought hard, trying to come up with a plan to save himself.

He was already running late, yet he lingered under a canopy of trees, soaking in the sun for a little while. He slept by the pond on the way; then he walked slowly towards the den.

In the meantime, the lion roared from his den, growing angry and impatient with every passing second. He saw the teeny-tiny rabbit enter his den and flew into a rage. 'Have I waited all day for this puny little creature? These animals ... I am going to hunt and kill now! How dare they send this tiny rabbit as my meal.'

Despite being scared, the rabbit remained calm. He mustered up his courage and said, 'Oh! My Majesty, the animals sent six rabbits today. But do you know what happened on the way? A ferocious-looking lion appeared and blocked our path. He claimed to be the new king of this forest!

'Whaaaaat!' the lion roared back.

The rabbit quivered. 'My Majesty, we told him we already have a brave lion as our king. But he growled in anger and kept the five rabbits with him. He then asked me to inform you that you must leave the forest at once, or he will kill you!'

The lion was furious and asked the rabbit to lead him to this new lion's den. 'I am going to kill this lion!'

The rabbit led the lion to a deep well.

When the lion looked inside the well, he saw his reflection in the water. But he thought it was the other lion. He let out a furious roar. He heard the echo of his voice and mistook the voice to be the other lion's.

The lion jumped inside the well to kill his enemy. But his head crashed against the rocks as he fell into the water and drowned. The little rabbit rushed back to tell the other animals that the forest was free of the terror of the greedy lion.

4. THE WISE PIGEON

Long ago, in a deep, dense jungle full of small lakes and lush green trees, there lived a flock of pigeons. Every morning, they flew together in the sky, chirping away merrily, looking for water, seeds, grains, earthworms and insects to eat. Every day, before nightfall the pigeons returned to their cosy nests in the jungle. A wise, old pigeon perched atop a tree watched them from afar and looked out for them.

One day, the flock of pigeons was on their way to find their favourite berries and greens and found a lot of rice grains scattered on the grass. The pigeons cooed excitedly and at once decided to fly to the ground to feed on the rice. The wise pigeon grew alert at once. 'So much rice in the forest! This is clearly a trap, my dears.' The wise pigeon thought that this was a trap in disguise laid down by a sly bird-catcher. He flew with great speed from the top of his tree to stop all the other pigeons before they reached the grass. But the hungry pigeons did not pay attention to the wise pigeon and got busy munching on the delicious snack.

The wise pigeon was right; the flock of pigeons were caught in a trap laid down by a bird-catcher.

'Oh no! My feet are entangled in the net. I can't move!' one of the pigeons cried out.

The bird-catcher was ecstatic at the sight of the restless pigeons trapped in his net. 'Ah! This is a bonanza! So many pigeons. I will cage them and sell them for a hefty price in the

market! Hurray!' he laughed and started to run towards the pigeons trapped in the net.

From the branch of a nearby tree, the wise pigeon saw the bird-catcher sprinting towards the pigeons. The pigeons did everything they could to free themselves. They pulled the net in all directions shrieking loudly.

'What do we do now? How do we break free from this net?' they cried in unison.

'Help! Please save us. You were right; we should have listened to you!' they begged the wise pigeon.

The wise pigeon asked them to stop pulling the net. 'Here's an idea—try flying upwards together. If you do so, you will be able to fly along with the net,' he advised.

The pigeons did as they were told. They started flapping their wings in unison. In a few minutes, the flock flew even though the net was still stuck to their feet.

The bird-catcher was shocked at the sight of a united flock of pigeons flying away with his net. He was left stumped in his boots. The wise pigeon led the flock, along with the net, to a mouse's place who was the wise pigeon's friend. The mouse welcomed the flock. The wise pigeon narrated the turmoil the flock had been through and requested him to help.

Although the mouse did not have wings to fly, he had a tool that the pigeons did not have—his sharp teeth. The mouse set to work and cut the entire net in no time, allowing all the pigeons to break free and touch the sky once again!

The pigeons thanked the mouse and the wise pigeon for helping them. 'Thank you! What would we do without both of you and your help,' they cried.

The wise pigeon responded, 'Unity is your best weapon against evil. Stay together! As long as you stay united, no harm can touch you.'

5. THE HUNGRY JACKAL

Once in a faraway forest that was home to many animals and birds, there lived a jackal. The jackal was perpetually hungry, no matter how much he ate. He was often found under a tree eating this and that, or sometimes under the twinkling stars feasting on insects, reptiles, fruits and fish. Soon, all the animals began to hide their food from the jackal. The animals were constantly worried about the jackal stealing their food and munching on everything in sight with his curved canines.

As all the animals began to eat their food in secret, there came a day when he couldn't find any food. The jackal was ravenous. He couldn't think on an empty stomach. He decided to visit the adjacent village. He reached a village full of colourful huts. Outside a yellow hut, little children played hopscotch under a big banyan tree. The door to the yellow hut was ajar, and an old lady came out. She called out to one child. 'Raju, I have made some rice and jaggery kheer for you.'

The jackal's mouth began watering. 'Oh! I want that pudding. I want it now!' he thought.

The jackal quickly hid behind the bushes. But the old woman, Raju's grandmother noticed the cunning jackal behind the hut. 'Raju beta, come inside for the pudding soon and be careful.'

Raju nodded and played until dark. Meanwhile, the jackal grew impatient, waiting for darkness to descend. He smirked as he planned to go inside the hut and attack the rice pudding. 'Yummy in my tummy!' he thought to himself.

Little did the jackal know that Raju's grandmother had cooked up a plan to get rid of him. As the sunset gave way to darkness, the grandmother watched the jackal grow restless behind the bushes. She walked inside the hut thinking hard. She smiled. 'I will teach that greedy jackal a lesson.' She placed a large pot of water on the stove to boil, then peeped outside the hut and called out to Raju 'Come beta, it's getting dark.'

The jackal came out from behind the bushes; he crept up to Raju's hut and hid behind the gate. He could hear the grandmother and child talk.

'Grandma, what is this large hole in our kitchen ceiling for?' asked Raju, surprised.

'The hole will let fresh air into the hut, my dear,' she said.

Raju was worried. 'I hope no animal enters our home.'

His grandmother told him not to worry.

The jackal's smile widened—a hole in the kitchen ceiling was the answer to his prayers.

'I can't believe my ears!' He swiftly climbed to the roof of the house. As he approached the hole, he felt a sense of relief. 'This is so easy! I will just lie down on the roof and wait for them to sleep, then that pudding will be in my tummy!'

Soon, the hungry jackal heard snoring from inside the hut. He stood up and jumped into the hole. As soon as he jumped, he fell into the pot of boiling water. 'Ouuuuuuuuuch!'

The jackal shrieked in pain and ran out of the hut.

The sight of a jackal running made Raju and his grandmother laugh. They both sat down to savour a hearty serving of Raju's grandmother's delicious pudding!

6. THE ELEPHANT AND THE DOG

Long, long ago there lived a king who loved all animals. He had an especially deep affection for elephants; he doted on the affable animals and fed them, hugged them and spent lots of time with them in the forest nearby. Alongside his grand palace, he built a very large stable for his royal elephant, Gopi. The king appointed a caretaker to look after Gopi; the caretaker fed fresh fruits and vegetables to Gopi during the day.

Once, when the caretaker was asleep, a stray dog entered the royal stable to find Gopi asleep under the shade of a large, leafy tree. The dog was hungry and searching for food. He appeared frail and bony and was about to give up on his search when suddenly he spotted some food by the tree. It was Gopi's leftover meal: soft rotis and milk. The dog ate it up. Gopi woke up and found a dog running around happily; Gopi smiled watching the joyful dog bounce from here to there. 'You can have my food every day, friend,' Gopi called out. Soon, both the animals became great friends. The dog now lived in the stable with Gopi and the caretaker didn't seem to mind it. Soon, the dog became healthy.

One day, a farmer approached the royal stable. He saw the dog and thought to himself: 'This dog will be good for protecting my farm; he looks strong.' The farmer asked the caretaker if he would sell the dog to him. The caretaker hesitated at first, but

when the farmer offered good money for the dog, the caretaker became greedy and accepted the money. He gave the dog to the farmer, although the dog did not belong to the caretaker.

The next morning Gopi looked everywhere for the dog. He cried sitting under the tree. 'I miss you!' The royal elephant Gopi missed his friend dearly. There was no one to play with; no one to share food with; no one to laugh and run with. Soon, Gopi became sad, and he refused to eat or drink or play.

The elephant lost interest in his day-to-day activities; he became weak. The news of Gopi's failing health reached the king, and he rushed to the royal stable to enquire.

The caretaker's face reddened; he was aware of why the elephant was so miserable and was declining food and water, but he did not speak up. He feared the king. 'My God! If the king finds out I sold Gopi's friend, a dog, who was not rightfully mine, I will be punished,' he thought and decided to keep quiet and feign ignorance.

The king was upset by Gopi's lack of interest in life. The royal vet was called to examine Gopi. The vet was unable to diagnose the cause of Gopi's failing health. 'It appears Gopi has grown emotional about a certain matter; his sorrow is apparent.'

The king's guards spoke with the helpers to find out what was wrong with Gopi.

Finally, the truth came out. Some of the helpers had seen the dog who lived with the elephant in the stable and was his close companion. The king summoned his people and announced that whoever found the dog would be rewarded with gold coins. The farmer upon hearing this, took the dog to the king and revealed the story about how the caretaker of the royal stable had sold him the dog.

The caretaker was called immediately. He confessed to selling the dog. The king then asked the caretaker to return the money to the farmer and take care of Gopi as well as the dog. Both the animals now lived happily in the stable. Gopi's health and smiles returned and the king was pleased.

7. THE TORTOISE AND THE GEESE

In a forest far away, there was a deep, blue pond full of aquatic life. A tortoise and two geese lived there; they were the best of friends and loved playing together by the shimmering pond in the bright daylight. Stories of their friendship grew far and wide among creatures of the pond.

The forest soon witnessed a dry spell. A drought struck the rivers, ponds and seas. Animals fell prey to the drought and even the humans began dying due to the lack of water. The geese found themselves starving and unable to sustain themselves. 'There's nothing here, our beautiful blue pond has dried,' the geese said one day while looking for fish. 'It's time to leave this forest and fly away to another place,' the other geese added.

Through some friends at sea, the geese heard of a place that had flowing water, full of fresh fish that would fill their bellies. They walked up the shore to say goodbye to their dear friend, the tortoise.

The tortoise's heart sank at the news of being left all alone. 'Please don't leave me. You are my friends. I can't live without you both.'

The geese were heartbroken too. They said, 'We don't want to leave you behind. But what can we do? We must eat to live.'

'You can go for many days without food and water, but sadly we can't.'

'Only if you had wings!'

But the tortoise had no wings and he could not fly.

The tortoise wept. 'Please, my lovelies. Take me along.'

Finally, the geese gave in. The tortoise agreed to a risky plan.

They told the tortoise: 'It's a good thing you have strong jaws.'

The geese looked around and found a stick; then they held the ends of the stick with their beaks. Finally, they asked the tortoise to hold the middle of the stick with his mouth. 'You must not speak or you will fall from the sky onto the face of the earth and hit your head.'

The tortoise grew alert; he knew this plan was full of danger. But he did not want to be left behind. He promised to remain silent during the flight.

The next day the geese flew into the sky, carrying the tortoise with them. The tortoise, for the first time in his life, felt the cool rush of air and saw the earth from above. Together, they flew over the prairies, fields, hills, forests and even a village.

The village was full of people going about their business. The village folk looked up to find two geese carrying a tortoise on a stick! They were amused: 'How shocking, the geese have captured the poor animal.'

The geese paid no heed and continued their journey flying between clouds. The tortoise, however, did not like this talk. He hated all the people pointing and staring in unison. He couldn't refrain from responding in an angry tone: 'You fools ...'

As he opened his mouth, he lost hold of the stick and fell from the skies onto the earth. Why did I open my mouth?' SMASH! He fell and never walked or talked again.

8. THE CAT'S CALL

Once in a thick forest full of open canopies, there lived a partridge, a small bird with a round body. The bird lived in a cosy nest underneath a large banyan tree. The nest had been home to the partridge for many years now. Lately, it had become common for the partridge to find her favourite snacks within the woods: insects, grains, corn and sunflower seeds. But the bird decided to travel to another place to hunt for food. She flew, gliding swiftly, showing off her chestnut tail. Finally, she reached a cornfield and stayed there for many days, devouring corn.

In the meantime, a rabbit came to live in the woods and made the partridge's nest his own. He lay in the nest and slept soundly after hopping around the woods all day long. When the partridge came home she was surprised to see that her home had been captured by a rabbit. 'Move on please, This is my home,' she said to the rabbit.

The rabbit did not quite like the partridge's behaviour. 'This is no longer your home. I found it empty when I got here. It's mine now.'

The rabbit and the partridge argued loudly for some time. Many animals from around the woods gathered and heard both sides of the argument. They were fed up with the constant yelling. 'It's better to take this matter to the judge,' they told the fighting animals.

The partridge and rabbit decided to travel to the banks of a holy river to find a solution to their problem.

When they reached, they froze in fear as they watched a scary-looking tomcat offering wisdom to other cats. How would they approach the wicked tomcat? He would eat them instantly. Both the rabbit and the partridge ignored the feeling of terror in their tummies and started bickering once again.

The tomcat, fully aware of its visitors, stood up on his hind legs and began to pray loudly. The partridge and the rabbit couldn't believe eyes—the sight of a holy cat impressed them. 'Looks like this pious tomcat won't do us any harm,' said the rabbit.

The partridge nodded. They both gingerly walked towards the praying tomcat. He opened his eyes and asked, 'How can I help you?'

The animals started arguing about their situation once again. The tomcat listened for a moment and then said with great conviction: 'My dear friends, you have travelled a long way to settle this. But you need to speak loudly, I am old and hard of hearing. Come closer and start from the beginning.'

By now, both the partridge and the rabbit trusted the tomcat and moved closer, in anticipation of finally resolving the issue of their house. As soon as they moved forward, the cat pounced, killed, and ate them instantly.

9. THE BLUE JACKAL

In a dense, lush jungle, where the trees swayed to the tunes of the wind and whispered the sound 'shhhhh', there lived a wily jackal. The jackal was always on the lookout for small creatures. One day, his hunger led him beyond the jungle into the heart of a village. As he ran, his cunning eyes kept looking out for any kind of food. The jackal's entry into the village drew a pack of dogs to him. The angry lot surrounded him and asked him to leave at once. They attacked him and tried to drive him away. The jackal leaped away to save himself from the ferocious dogs and ran into a house nearby. 'Oh God! Where am I?' the jackal wondered. He looked for a place to hide while the dogs continued to growl outside the house.

It was a washerman's house—the front yard of the house was full of giant tubs. Shirts, pants and other pieces of clothing were hung out to dry on a clothesline. The jackal was almost out of breath from the running and leaping. He noticed a humongous vat and jumped into it to hide from the pack of wicked dogs. The dogs looked everywhere for the jackal but couldn't find him anywhere.

The giant vat in which he had been hiding was full of blue dye. Moreover, just as he emerged from the vat, he knocked over another small container of blue dye! The jackal's whole body was now all blue.

The dogs, upon seeing this strange blue creature, grew curious. 'Who is this blue creature? He looks frightening!' The dogs ran for their life.

The jackal was happy that the dogs now feared him. He walked like a king into the forest, scaring all the animals away. 'Ha! Ha! Ha! Who wants to mess with me?' He yelled at the top of his voice. The forest grew silent. All the animals, big and small, were terrified of this blue creature.

The jackal crossed a river in the jungle, ate a hearty meal and then looked at his reflection. 'Oh! The silly animals are afraid of my colour! Little do they know it is a dye. Hahaha!' he laughed.

Just then an idea occurred to him. He went atop a hill in the village and called out to all the animals of the forest. 'Listen up! My dear friends. I am your new king. The Almighty—the creator of this jungle—has sent me from the skies above to protect you.'

All the animals gathered: rabbits, squirrels, elephants, foxes, sheep, goats, and even a lion and a few tigresses with their cubs attended the meeting. They seemed convinced and bowed to the Blue King. They followed every instruction the jackal issued. 'Go, and chase away all the jackals out of this jungle. They are a big threat to our kingdom,' he ordered them. The animals did what they were asked to do. Next, the jackal asked the animals to drive away the pack of dogs from the village. 'They are useless! Throw them out of our kingdom.'

The animals spent all day bringing the jackal food and water and looking after his needs, growing weary by the minute.

A few days passed. One day the jackal was speaking to all the animals gathered, dishing out instructions. He heard a sound. A familiar, comforting sound from afar. A pack of jackals stood howling in the forest close by. The jackal's heart lit up. He

had been away from his kind for too long. A wave of happiness rushed over him. He forgot where he was and joined the call of the jackals, howling in response.

The jackal kept howling 'Owwww' with his kind, feeling a sense of thrill in his chest. The other animals were shocked. Their mouths fell open. 'The blue creature is just a wily jackal. He fooled us and how!' the lion roared.

The jackal shivered as all the animals chased him away from their jungle and the village.

10. THE GREEDY BIRD

In a dense forest, a flock of birds lived among the trees near a tranquil lake. The flock of birds was happy, looking out for each other. An old queen bird supervised this flock. Every day, as the sun shone in the sky, the queen bird would flutter her feathers and call to her flock. She would then divide the birds into small groups and send them to fetch food from different directions.

The birds liked working under their queen. They worked hard all day, returning to their nests in the tree and bringing their finds of the day. Often, if a bird found a patch of grass with too many seeds or grains, it would beckon the rest of the group to help carry all the food back to the nest.

At dusk, all the birds would chirp away merrily, munching on insects, grains, leaves, bits of bread and pumpkin seeds. The queen bird ensured all the birds got an equal share, and no bird slept hungry. The birds looked forward to gathering in the evening, exchanging stories of the day and spending time with the flock.

One cloudy day, a young bird on its expedition for food reached a crowded village. She noticed many villagers busy farming, tending to their homes and carrying out a flurry of other activities. Bullock carts carried sacks of food grains from

the fields to the city market. The young bird picked the grains that had fallen off the cart and onto the road.

The bird's stomach rumbled at the sight of so much food. A sense of greed came over her. 'Wow! This spread is so yummy. I spotted these grains—they belong to me now. I am not sharing this food with anyone.'

Her greedy mind cooked up a plan. She flew back to forest and told the queen bird about the village road strewn with fresh grains, overflowing from the carts on their way to the market.

'But ...' the queen warned.

'But, what?' said the young bird in a worried voice.

'... All this food could be ours, but unfortunately, it's rather unsafe to fly down the road to peck at the grains. There are plenty of carts on the road and they move dangerously,' the queen explained. 'I worry any bird trying to pick at the grains may get crushed under the carts driven by the bullocks. I think it best if no bird flies in that direction.'

The queen bird instructed the flock to stay away from the treacherous road in the village. The young bird could hardly contain her excitement; all the grains were hers to eat. She would watch the incoming carts as she pecked at the grains. The young bird smiled with confidence in her agility.

Every day, the young bird flew discreetly to the village and relished the grains alone. Now, her days did not count for effort or teamwork. No movement—just food. The young bird slowly grew into this habit of indulging without flying around.

Soon, the young bird grew very fat. She lost the ability to fly and move due to her excess weight. One day, as the young bird got busy pecking at a fresh batch of grains, she failed to notice a cart moving towards her. In minutes, the bullock cart crushed the young bird under its wheels.

11. FOUR FRIENDS AND A HUNTER

Long, long ago, in a forest by a deep lake, there lived four best friends: a mouse, a deer, a crow and a tortoise. The four animals were often seen playing by the lake, chasing each other and feasting on food together. Over the years their friendship became strong. They knew they could rely on each other.

One day, the animals were lazing around on the warm grass under a balmy sun, telling each other about their day's adventures. They heard footsteps on the grass and turned around to see a hunter approaching them with a trap. The deer sprang to its feet and ran into the woods, the crow flew up into the sky, soaring to the top of the trees, and the mouse moved swiftly, darting into a hole by the lake. They fled, escaping the hunter.

The hunter gave a big sigh of disappointment. The deer, the crow and the mouse had darted away from his grasp. But the the tortoise, despite his efforts, had only managed to inch slowly away from him. The hunter took hold of the tortoise. 'Caught you!' he laughed, walking away.

The hunter looked forward to eating the tortoise for dinner. Meanwhile, the deer, the mouse and the crow became worried for their friend. 'We must think of a plan to save our friend soon,' the deer told his friends. The crow and the mouse agreed. The crow took off into the sky to find the hunter. The deer found the hunter through the crow's signal and overtook

him with great speed. He went and lay down at a little distance on the grass, pretending to be dead.

The hunter was ecstatic. 'Hurray!' He dropped the net carrying the tortoise to get closer to the deer. At that moment, the mouse slithered from his hole and into action. He chewed on the net and set the tortoise free!

Both the tortoise and the mouse scuttled away and hid from the hunter. The hunter, by now, had forgotten all about the tortoise, as he greedily focused on the deer. As soon as he touched the deer, the deer sprang to life and bolted into the woods, back to his friends.

The hunter, now angry, went back to get the tortoise but to his dismay, the tortoise was nowhere to be found.

The four friends celebrated the tortoise's escape from the hunter! Their friendship had saved their lives.

12. THE ELEPHANT WHO WANTED TO MAKE FRIENDS

Once upon a time, an elephant was sitting under a banyan tree in a dense forest, feeling lonely. After a while, he decided to walk along the forest path and make some friends. He swayed his trunk and stomped along the path for a long time. Eventually, he found a canopy of green leafy trees and sat underneath it. He prayed to God: 'Dear God, please send some animals my way so I can play with them.' Almost instantly, a monkey appeared. The elephant smiled and called out to the monkey: 'Hello! Will you be my friend, Monkey?'

The monkey responded, 'Aren't you too big to swing on trees like me? I can't be your friend.' The elephant felt glum; he strode ahead and came across a rabbit who was busy digging a tunnel.

The elephant asked the rabbit if he would be his friend. The rabbit replied promptly. 'You see this burrow, it's so tiny. You, dear elephant, are large, you will never be able to fit in my burrow. How can we become friends then?'

A few hours later, the elephant met a frog who was busy eating insects. The elephant asked the frog if they could be friends. The frog responded: 'I will be your friend if you can hop like me! Can you?' The elephant shook his head, his trunk swinging from side to side. The frog hopped away saying: 'Sorry!'

Next, the elephant met a fox, who declined his friendship as well. Tired after a long and sad day, the elephant went to sleep by the lake.

The next day, he awoke to a lot of noise. The forest animals were running helter-skelter in fear. The elephant stopped a deer that was bolting through the trees and asked about the chaos. 'There's a tiger, and he is going on a rampage. I have to run! He has killed many animals already!'

The deer, the bear, the sheep and the goat were all running like the forest were on fire. Soon, the tiger appeared, looking ferocious. The elephant's heart sank at the sight of animals running around in panic trying to save themselves.

'Please ... please Sir, you are the mightiest. Have mercy on the animals and leave them alone. Please don't kill them,' cried the elephant.

The tiger, angrier now, told the elephant to get out of his way. 'What are you going to do? Stop me! Hahaha.' The elephant noticed the crowd of animals around him: the monkey, the rabbit, the fox and the frog were all out of breath. The elephant extended his mighty leg and kicked the tiger with all his strength. The tiger fell to the grass. Scared, he ran to the other side.

All the animals roared and cheered for the elephant. And then they hugged him with love. Together, they thanked him for getting rid of the tiger and said, 'You are perfect as you are! Please be our friend!'

The elephant was as happy as a lark. He had finally found friends to play with.

13. THE WISE PARROTS

Once, in a forest full of many animals like sparrows, pigeons, squirrels, and peacocks, lived two parrots who squealed and squawked together. They broke open nuts for meals by the lake and flew from tree to tree adding a dash of colour to the forest.

One warm summer evening, a hunter passed through the forest when he suddenly heard the parrots. He paused to look around and saw the two green parrots squawking and holding food with their feet. Their whistles and green feathers soothed the hunter's eyes and ears. He thought to himself, 'The king will be very pleased if I give these parrots to him. He will surely reward me!'

The hunter quietly laid a trap and caught the parrots. 'Help! Help!' the parrots squirmed uncomfortably in the trap. They screeched and whistled 'khi khi' but no one came to their rescue.

The hunter then gifted the parrots to the king of a vast kingdom who lived in a majestic palace. The king took great care of the parrots, spent time with them, fed them, played with them—he even let them fly in his garden full of flowers.

The parrots taught the king to mimic and screech like them. They were delighted to eat fresh fruits and all the other fancy food items prepared for them by the king's chef. The care and respect they received from the king made

them forget all about the forest, and the parrots made the king's palace their home.

'We are so loved here,' said one parrot to the other.

'Thank God for the hunter who brought us here!' agreed the other parrot.

The parrots soon became the centre of attention in the kingdom. They were loved by all the ministers and visitors.

Then came a day when everything changed.

The hunter returned to the palace and he did not come empty-handed. This time, he had another present for the king. The parrots saw that the hunter had brought the king a gorgeous black monkey. The monkey became a big hit. He garnered all the attention, love, care and respect that had been showered on the parrots earlier. Slowly, the king stopped visiting the parrots and spent all his free time with the monkey.

The parrots were sad—they felt neglected and helpless. 'I am heartbroken. No one cares for us now. No one even looks our way,' one parrot said and started to weep.

The other parrot became teary and replied, 'I know! It hurts. But don't worry friend! Nothing in the world is permanent. Everything changes. Life is fleeting.'

Some days passed and the parrots began thinking of flying to the forest, back to their own home. But the thought of leaving the palace and the king filled them with dread. Just then, they heard that the monkey had begun acting up and stirring trouble. He was hitting and scratching all those who visited him. He had even bitten someone. The monkey's behaviour was out of control.

The king feared seeing the monkey now, for the creature had become unpredictable. He ordered the hunter to carry the monkey back into the wild. 'He does not belong here.'

The parrots regained all the love and attention. 'Good times are here!' screeched one of the parrots who had been weeping.

'Times, they are always changing! We should hold on to our patience even when life seems unfavourable,' replied the wise, patient parrot.

14. THE LION AND THE BULLS

Once, in a jungle, a hungry lion had been watching three bulls feed on grass in an open field. The lion noticed that the bulls stayed together most of the time. Out and about in the morning sun, they roamed in a group, looking for a lake to quench their thirst. The lion approached them and with all his ferocity tried to attack the bulls, but the bulls came together in the face of this brutal attack and drove him away.

The bulls stood up for each other, shielding one another from harm and wild animals looking to hurt them.

The lion was hungry and salivating at the sight of bulls in the jungle, but he didn't know how to get to the bulls. The lion began dreaming of feasting on at least one bull. The bulls were, after all, strong with large muscular shoulders. 'I am no match for them. They have sharp horns and hard hooves—these bulls can seriously injure me!' the lion thought.

Still, the lion stayed close to the bulls, watching them from afar. He found it hard to keep away from such a good meal that was wandering along the open field!

One day, one of the bulls was in a bad mood. He wanted to graze in another field and started throwing a tantrum. The other two bulls did not like his tone. Soon, the three bulls started fighting amongst themselves. The lion watched them walk away from each other into three different corners of the field.

Realising that this was his chance, the lion pounced on one bull, then the next and finally the last one without any resistance or injury. He had taken advantage of the rift between the bulls. Togetherness had been their weapon. On their own, the bulls, no matter how strong, were easy to attack.

15. THE JACKAL AND THE DRUM

Far away in a forest full of birds and bees, elephants and sheep, there lived a greedy jackal. This jackal was lazy and he hated going out into the jungle and finding food. When hungry, he would eat animals killed by the other jackals who loathed this behaviour and excluded him from the pack.

Lonely and without any friends, the jackal now had to look for his food. He dreamt of small rabbits, insects, fruits and vegetables. His stomach rumbled from hunger and he started to scour the jungle for food.

Eventually, he wandered into a battleground. The air was thick with the smell of smoke. The terrain seemed like it had been deserted recently.

The jackal lingered near the battleground. Suddenly, he heard a loud, thundering sound. Frightened, he thought to himself 'Dear God! Where am I? Is that a monster? Who on earth can make such a scary sound?'

The earth-shattering sound kept ringing in his ears. The jackal shrivelled up in fear.

He thought that a dangerous creature was lurking close to him. He turned around. He started to flee the battlefield and run back to the woods when a thought struck him.

'That sound could have been anything? How do I know if it is a dangerous animal? It could be, but what if there isn't any animal?'

His head burned with these new possibilities. The jackal mustered up his courage and thought, 'It's silly to run away from an animal or monster without knowing what it is!'

The jackal went back to the battleground and inched closer to the sound, nervous that he might face a vicious animal.

But instead he encountered a giant war drum under a big banyan tree! The wind was making the branches hit the drum with immense force causing the ear-splitting sound.

'I was fearful of these dancing tree branches,' the jackal laughed at his silly and unwise ways.

Soon, the jackal, pumped up on his newfound courage, stumbled across a tent that was home to a large store of delicious food and clean water! The jackal thanked his stars and relished the food that he had found on his own, by overcoming his fear.

16. THE BABY QUAIL WHO COULD NOT FLY AWAY

Long, long ago, in a forest full of dry trees and parched grass, an enlightened soul was born as a tiny quail. The baby quail, with her small wings and little feet, was too young to fly or walk. She lived with her parents and three siblings in a cosy nest on a treetop under a bright blue sky. The trees in the tiny quail's neighbourhood shed their orange, red and yellow-coloured leaves at the turn of the season, leading to a burst of colour on the ground.

The leaves rustled as the baby quail's family scurried across them, searching for tasty insects and seeds. The little quail's parents lovingly fed their chick bits of food from their beaks. Mommy Quail carefully picked out the yummiest seeds for her little one, while Daddy Quail fed her every few hours. Their nest, perched on top of a dry deciduous tree, was abuzz with loud shrieks and the chip-chip-chip of the tiny quail.

Each year, the forest faced blazing fires that spread through the land, scorching trees, chasing away birds and bees, and sending rabbits, lizards, squirrels, deer, elephants, panthers, tigers, monkeys and many other animals scurrying for their lives. This year, too, after a particularly hot spell, the forest caught a rage of bursting flames. The forest was beginning to get very hot, as the foliage strewn on the forest floor crackled and burned. All the birds flew away. The tiny quail's parents looked after her, shielding her from the hot winds and fires as best as they could.

Soon, the fires reached the tree on which the little quail lived with her family. But she couldn't walk or fly yet. So, with tears in their eyes, the little bird's family was forced to abandon her. Her parents tried hard to carry her in their beaks, but it was impossible. The baby quail was left alone amidst the roaring fire. She was overwhelmed with helplessness as the crackling sound took over the forest. Tears welled up in her eyes as the wildfire burned everything in sight. 'I am all alone. I can't save myself,' she thought to herself.

But, the very next moment, a sense of clarity dawned upon her.

'My parents loved me deeply. Their unconditional love shielded me from harm at every step. Even when the fire broke out, they stayed by my side until the last minute.

'Only love is real. My parent's kindness is within me, in every beat of my tiny heart. Despite their best efforts, they were helpless to carry and save me. I pray and hope they are alive and well. I thank them for their love and generosity.'

The quail thought about how she was now all alone. 'No one is around to help me. My wings and feet cannot help me fly or walk. But this universe has gifted me with a thoughtful mind—a mind that has only known the boundless love and kindness of my dearest parents.

'I only have gratitude and innocent truthfulness in my heart. I feel pure love and joy through my veins for the life I have had so far.'

In that next moment, a miracle took place. A deep wisdom awakened within her, embracing her like a warm hug. Her innocence had led her to know who she truly was—her truth and the truth of her past lives. She became one with the universe—the entire consciousness embodied her. This realisation allowed the quail to learn that in her previous lifetime, she had

known pure compassion and love. As she connected with this deep wisdom, she felt grateful.

The enlightened being in the quail then made a wish. 'The universe is kind, and I wish it protects this land. May no harm or fire ever touch this place for a million years. May all creatures, plants, twigs, trees and insects caught in the fire be saved.'

As if the universe had been listening, the fire stopped suddenly. The flames and the smoke simply vanished into thin air. The baby quail was safe. The forest, the trees and all animals around her were safe, protected by the power of her pure and loving heart.

17. THE SNAKE AND THE EELS

Long ago, in the far-off Eastern Kingdom, there lived a king who took great pride in his kingdom's lush gardens and cool, calming ponds. Nature was the heart of the kingdom—trees bore green leaves, ancient willow trees danced with the winds, birds chirped in their nests, and fish and eels swam in tranquil, flowing waters under a balmy blue sky. Nature pierced the silence of the kingdom with its soft, gentle music. The gardens, full of natural charm, lured people to spend time by the shimmering pond, filled with delicate lotus blossoms.

One sunny morning, the king and his son, the prince, decided to stroll along the pond's edge. The prince was loved by all for his calm composure.

As they walked, they heard the rustle of leaves and the soft murmur of water lapping at the edge of the pond. The prince, struck by the resplendent greens that morning, wandered a little off the path and reached the water's edge.

The sight of the calming pond compelled him to step into the water. The king was pleased to see the prince relaxing and soaking in the sun. But at that moment, the prince felt an odd sensation running through his legs. A sleek snake emerged from the water and swiftly coiled around him. The king watched in horror as his beloved son writhed in pain under the snake's grip.

The king, driven by instinct, withdrew his sword and killed the snake. As its lifeless body slipped into the water, the king sat down, fear clouding his mind. The once-tranquil pond now seemed treacherous, clouded by dangers that lurked in its depths.

The king addressed his men in a stern voice. 'I want every snake in this pond eliminated,' he commanded, standing tall and resolute.

There was no hesitation in his voice. The safety of his son and the sanctity of his kingdom demanded swift action. All threats—real or imagined—had to be dealt with at the earliest. His men, eager to him, got to work at dawn.

In the early morning light, all the creatures of the pond—fish, snakes and eels—glided in fluid movements. The king's men peered into the water but struggled to clearly discern one creature from another. All they saw was a mass of sinuous forms. They couldn't identify the dangerous serpents from the harmless eels.

Unsure of what to do and pressurised by the king's urgent orders, the men resorted to killing all creatures with abandon. By the time, the waters fell still, the pond was emptied of life. The men took the lifeless bodies of snakes and eels to the king.

The king's heart grew heavy. His pond's once-thriving life lay still before him, no longer writhing or moving like it once did. The wicked snakes and the harmless eels both lay dead. The innocent eels, vital to the pond's health and ecosystem, had been slain for no reason. They had done no harm. They only protected the pond.

Tears welled in the king's eyes. He regretted his impulsive judgment and haste to kill the venomous snakes. 'The good have perished along with the evil,' he murmured.

But it was too late. His misguided zeal to protect his son had forever changed the kingdom's natural landscape.

18. THE BRAVE LITTLE PARROT

Once, in an age long past, the Buddha was reborn as a compassionate and caring little parrot. One fateful day, a storm burst through the skies and turned violent within minutes. Thunder swept through the parrot's cosy forest home. Lightning shrieked across the sky and lashed out in rumbling streaks, splitting the heavens. A withered tree trembled under the force of the thunder. Soon, a fiery bolt erupted into flames and struck the tree with all its might—CRACK!

The wind gained force—fiery sparks leaped on the wind, and in no time, the forest was ablaze. Cries of panic and fear spread as swiftly as the fire. All animals bolted for their lives as smoke engulfed the forest. A thick, choking smog emerged from all corners, threatening to destroy Mother Nature and its wildlife.

The little parrot, taken aback by the fiery storm, yelled, 'Fire! Help! Fire in our forest!' He flew to the nearby river, flapping his wings vigorously to escape the fury of the storm, now at its peak. But as he moved further away, he saw many deer, sheep, goats and myriad other animals trapped by the flames below. They cried and fought against the fury of the hot smoke but found no way to escape.

The parrot's heart ached at the sight of his friends caught in the fire. Then, he was struck by an idea. Immediately, he darted to the river, dipped into the cool waters and flew back to the now-raging fire.

The heat from the burning forest left him exhausted and breathless. The smog rising from the fire made it difficult for the parrot to breathe. The heat roasted his small body. Within minutes, humongous walls of flames arose. The fire crackled and lashed out from all corners, never resting for a moment. The little parrot glided, turned and dodged the furious flames. With bravery in his heart, he flew over the centre of the forest. He flapped his wings and shook them, releasing a few drops of water into the fiery forest. The tiny amount of water vanished into the blaze with a soft hisssssssssssss.

But the parrot refused to give up. Again and again, he flew to the river, dipped into the water and returned to sprinkle more drops into the flames, trying desperately to save his beloved home and friends. He felt dizzy; his head spun like a merry-go-round. His lungs burned from the thick fumes. His feet were scorched, his eyes bleary and red from the smoke.

The gods in the skies above watched the little parrot's struggle. 'It looks like he is being roasted in a hot oven,' one remarked. 'Ready to serve!' another added.

Their laughter roared through the upper realms of the spirit world, where all the devas and gods resided. As they lounged on soft, cushy clouds, listening to divine music and inhaling pure air, they exclaimed, 'The little parrot is indeed foolish. Look at him sprinkling water over raging forest flames. This is funny! Silly little parrot!' they laughed in unison.

One of the gods, however, was struck by the little parrot's hope. He uttered a few mantras and transformed himself into a golden eagle. Moved by the little parrot's sacrifice, this great eagle, with big golden eyes, flapped his wings and flew down towards the parrot.

He approached the little parrot, who was nearly black and charred from the fires.

'Little parrot, your efforts are futile. Your few tiny drops of water cannot and will not douse this beast of a fire! Go, get some respite and recover before it's too late for you,' the great eagle said in an intimidating tone.

But the words did not shake the parrot's resolve. He continued to fly back and forth through the flames. The golden eagle's giant eyes grew twice their size as he yelled, 'Stop! Stop at once! Go save yourself!'

The little parrot responded with a long, wheezing cough and said, 'Your advice—I don't need it.' Cough, cough, splatter, shriek. The little parrot struggled to speak through muffled coughs. 'You are a big, shining eagle! You can help, but you are not helping—only advising. What good are your words when my beloved home is burning to ashes?'

The god, in the body of the magnificent eagle, was moved by the little parrot's unwavering determination. His eyes darted to the other gods sitting above, devouring delicious fruits and soaking in unfiltered sunlight. They laughed and joked with reckless abandon, while on Earth, animals cried in panic and fear. As the gods danced and sang, so many suffered below.

The great being's heart melted, and he felt ashamed. A deep longing to help, like the little parrot, arose within him. He, a god with unlimited powers, had done nothing. Tears welled in his golden eyes—huge, shimmering tears. As they fell, they poured down like cool, sparkling rain over the blazing forest. Wave after wave, the magical tears, cascaded over the flames, until, at last, the forest was safe once more.

The little parrot beamed with joy and let out a triumphant shriek. Clean and bright from the magical rain, he flew through the fresh, glistening sky. 'Thank you, Eagle! This is the kind of help I meant!'

Soon, blades of grass sprouted, fresh and vibrant, ready to paint the forest with love and life once again.

Each shimmering teardrop transformed into new feathers on the parrot's wings. Red, yellow and green burst forth in a brilliant display, making him more radiant than ever!

The animals looked at each other in wonder—they were unharmed, whole and one with nature. Above them, in the sunny skies, their small but fearless friend, the little parrot, soared with pure joy. He had not relented when hope seemed bleak and persisted in saving his home despite the odds. He had saved them when all seemed lost.

A chorus of shrieks rang out: 'Hurray for the brave little parrot! Hurray for the miraculous rain!'

19. THE LITTLE SPARROW AND THE BIG SEA

Once, a long time ago, in the middle of the wilderness, there lived a little sparrow and his friend. They loved spending time together. Their home was nestled within a big apple tree that bore juicy apples during winter. They liked to hop along whispering trees, squabble over insects, seeds and grains, and fly over a small pond that shimmered under a bright yellow sun and twinkled with a luminescent glow beneath a full moon on nights filled with the crick-crick sounds of crickets.

The pond was their favourite place. They hopped by the pond's edge and watched orange and yellow fish swim in its cool, clean water. Frogs leaped, flies and dragonflies hovered above and bees buzzed. The sparrow and his mate spent their days by the pond, dipping their beaks and drinking from the water now and then.

One day, a thought struck the sparrow. He said to his mate: 'This pond here by our home is too small. I don't see too many fish. It's been the same old thing. The water is quite low. It's not enough, dear!'

His mate nodded.

The sparrow ruffled his body and wings and continued, 'How about we live someplace where the water runs deep and cool? Where there's infinite water, and where we can glug as much water as we like!'

'And where might such a place be?' his mate asked.

The sparrow squealed, 'The sea! It's vast. Imagine endless waves rolling before us as we dip and drink. It's time to say adios to this baby pond and go see the infinite sea.'

So they set off, flying over mountains and prairies, over wild geese, over fields with farmers, and over monkeys jumping on trees, over rivers sparkling under a golden sun, until they finally reached their destination—the vast, endless sea.

The sparrow and his mate looked out as far as they could and saw the splashing sea and heard the rhythmic waves. The air thick with salt wafted through their senses.

'It's all for us!' the sparrow cried.

He got to work, hopped close to the edge, bent down quickly and dipped his beak into the sea. After a few minutes, the sparrow lifted its brown body and heaved a big sigh. His mate expected him to drink for a long, long time without stopping.

'You drank as much as you did at the pond. Didn't you come here to quench your thirst from the infinite stretch of this never-ending sea?'

The sparrow's belly was full of water. He fluffed his feathers and took a deep breath. He replied with a hint of pride, 'Well, I could drink up the whole sea, you know! But this water—it's brackish, too salty for my taste!'

His mate chuckled. She realised the sparrow believed the sea would offer something the pond didn't. But that wasn't the case. The truth dawned on her: the sea in all its vastness didn't matter—for the ability and the appetite for water stayed the same.

The two sparrows made a new home by the sea but with a newfound learning—no matter how grand or big a place may seem, one's nature stays the same.

20. THE OWL AND THE ECHO

Many years ago, an owl named Olie lived in a jungle full of sparrows, pigeons, hummingbirds, bluebirds, cuckoos and other lovely birds who pecked and chirped happily. The jungle, with its thick green canopies and bushes, often buzzed with the sweet songs of the birds during the day.

Olie was a little vain and took great pride in the majestic appearance he saw in the deep blue lake now and then. His big, round dark eyes glowed like bulbs in the night, and his feathers were starry like the galaxies stirring in the night sky. But he was most impressed with his barks and whistles, his coos and hisses. Olie was in love with the sound of his hooting. Olie thought his voice was as sweet as the bunch of grapes that hung from his favourite tree.

Every night, as the moon cast its luminous glow over the treetops, Olie would fly to his favourite part of the jungle, perch in the hollow of his favourite oak tree, and hoot and hiss and scream as loudly as he could. 'Hooo—heeee—hooooo!' he shrieked with glee, all the while thinking his voice was akin to honey melting in a cup of warm milk.

'These woods are so lucky to hear my songs! I know for sure Mother Nature loves my songs!'

Immediately, a mysterious voice echoed back: 'Nature loves my songs!'

Olie's happiness and pride knew no bounds. His chest puffed up with joy.

'I knew it! A-ha—I just knew it! I think the nightingale must hand over her position as the most melodious singer to Olie, the awesome singer!'

'Olie, the awesome singer!' the voice repeated.

Turns out, Olie didn't realise that the voice he heard was only an echo of his own sound. He thought an admirer in the forest was praising him. Olie took this flattery as proof that the world needed to hear more of his sugary voice—all day and all night.

Just as the sun brightened the forest sky, the birds awoke and cheered each other with their sweet good mornings. The robins, magpies, sparrows and larks filled the forest with a beautiful melody of serene music.

Olie joined in with his hiss and hooting. He went on—unstoppable! But his loud, uninterrupted sounds did not delight the birds as he'd expected. The birds grew angry and upset at his mournful, almost tragic, wails.

They tried to shut out the noise by flying away, but the hoots followed them across mountains and over distant treetops—there was no escaping it! The blue jays squawked to protest, and the crows came together and shook their heads in alarm.

'This is dreadful!' chirped the hummingbirds.

'The song of the morning is sweet and soft. We need to tell Olie to quiet down!' tweeted the robins.

'Make it stop!' cried the morning larks.

The birds met to find a solution. They chirped and squealed in unison to annoy Olie. They all swooped down upon him, pecking and giving him a proper scolding.

Olie was a little injured. His feathers were ruffled and worn from the birds' collective strike. His pride had taken a hit too. His vanity bruised, he hurried past trees and lakes back to his hollowed oak tree.

The birds chased him, crying out, 'Hoot only at night! Mornings are for songs of peace and light!'

From that day on, Olie learned to keep his hiss and hooting for the nighttime when the world was dark and quiet. He ensured his voice did not bother any other bird or animal in the woods.

So Olie continued to sing his songs to the moon, the stars, and the distant galaxies scattered across the black sky. He still loved and believed in his special melody but never again mistook his echo for the voice of praise.

21. THE DONKEY AND THE WATCHDOG

Years ago, a donkey and a loyal watchdog lived in the same flooded fields where rice plants grew. The farmer tended to his paddy lovingly during the day, and at night, the watchdog patrolled the fields, looking for danger.

As the stars lit up the night sky, the watchdog got to work. 'Woof! Woof! Wooooof!' His bark was peculiar and sounded scary to everyone who heard it. Thieves, jolted by the noise, turned around and left without stealing a thing.

The watchdog was brave and did his best to protect the paddy field that was his home.

One quiet evening, under a faint moon, the donkey lay awake—bored and restless. A few minutes later, he heard the watchdog bark. A thought struck him: 'Isn't that fun! I want to try it too.'

He got excited, lifted his head, and brayed, 'Heee-haw! Heee-haw!' all through the evening and into the night. His braying picked up speed and grew louder. The annoying sound echoed across the village. It woke up people, badgered the cows and the chickens, and eventually disturbed the grumpy old farmer.

The next morning, the farmer saw the donkey sleeping like a log. He looked worn out from all the braying.

'Dear God! My poor donkey—he looks exhausted. He must be sick. No wonder he made such a terrible noise last night!'

The farmer scratched his head and called the village doctor. The doctor arrived with his white bag full of tools to inspect the animal. He ran his hands through his patient's mane, looked deep into his bulging eyes and made a serious face. The farmer grew worried.

The doctor said gravely, 'This is worse than I thought. If we don't act quickly, the donkey could fall really sick! The only cure is to give him an injection and then chase him with a thorny branch every few hours.'

The donkey brayed again, this time out of fear and worry. 'I am not sick. I was only joking—I wanted to have fun like the watchdog,' he pleaded.

The doctor shook his head. 'The illness has gone to his head. He is now hallucinating and telling stories. We need to treat him now!'

The donkey wanted to leap and run, but it was too late. Before he could say another word, the farmer and the doctor gathered the village folk and surrounded the donkey with sharp branches and sticks in their hands, yelling and screaming all the while. The donkey was overwhelmed and wished to run for his life but could see no way out.

After a few days when the donkey was finally on his own, he ran into the watchdog. The donkey looked tired and was recovering from being chased down by a dozen angry men. It was a bright, sunny day, and the dog was strolling through the field, ready to tuck himself by a rock.

'What happened, my friend? You look miserable,' asked the dog, wagging his tail.

The donkey heaved a big sigh and hung his head low.

'I thought barking was fun and games. I wanted to bark like you to kill my boredom. But instead I got into big trouble! I have learned my lesson now.'

The watchdog looked at his friend's sorry state and couldn't help chuckling.

'What works for me might not work for you, my friend. It's better to find your way to have fun, without causing so much chaos and pain!'

The donkey learned there was no point in copying others. He found joy in being his true self. He learned to busy himself grazing lazily, rolling in the fields and munching on sweet, juicy carrots.

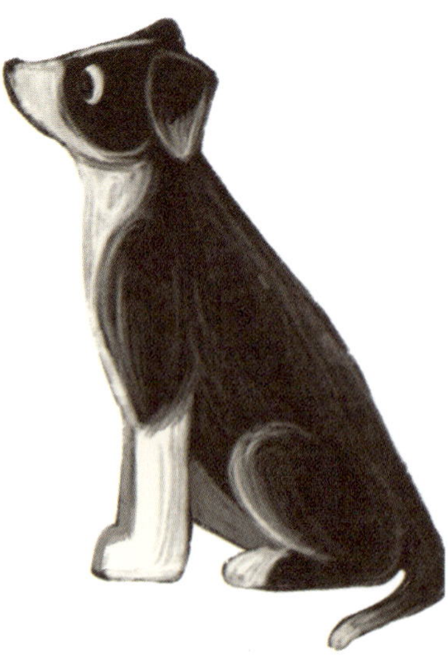

22. THE OLD TIGER AND THE GENTLE GIRAFFE

Once, in a jungle, there lived a tiger named Old Guile. He was much too old and weak to run after sheep, deer, goats or any of the animals he once hunted for a wholesome meal.

One hot day when the sun streamed through branches, casting a patchwork of shadows, he lay beneath a big shady tree—hungry and ready to eat whoever that crossed his path.

Just then, a jolly giraffe named Tall Stripes approached the lake for a drink. The day was windless and hot. Not a single leaf fluttered. Old Guile spotted this delicious-looking meal walking by merrily.

He called out, 'Hello! This horrid, hot day just took a turn for the better. Aren't you the son of my dear old friend, Yellow Haunch?'

Tall Stripes turned around in surprise. 'You know my father? That is quite astonishing—a tiger and a giraffe friends?'

Old Guile's forehead gleamed with sweat, and his eyes looked alert. He replied cheerily, 'My dear boy, you are not in on this big secret. Tigers and giraffes are practically family. Look at your long frame—you have golden fur, just like me. And, don't get me started on our stripes! They are so similar, it's hard to miss.'

Tall Stripes, being innocent and good-hearted, was touched by the tiger's words.

'Wow! I had no clue. This is brand-new information!'

Saddened by the tiger's weak state, the giraffe asked, 'Would you like me to bring you something?'

Old Guile gave a soft roar and shook his head. 'You are so kind. But I have passed my prime. I spend my days by this shimmering lake, thinking about life and death. My end is near. Do drop by and spend time with me again soon.'

Tall Stripes smiled and nodded. 'I will be there soon, Uncle Guile!'

He turned to leave but the tiger sighed.

'My dearest, life for me is uncertain. I might not be here tomorrow. Before you go, won't you come close and tell me a little about your father? It's been so long....'

Tall Stripes was moved. Without thinking too much, he leaned his long frame and sat by the old tiger.

SNAP!

The tiger roared to life and dug his sharp claws into the giraffe's neck.

Tall Stripes, unaware of Old Guile's treacherous ways, lay there—dead. He was still and silent.

That hot day, the tiger got the meal he'd wished for—not by hunting but through trickery and lies.

23. THE PIGS AND THE SAGE

One fine morning, a happy group of little pigs oinked their way to a bubbling brook. The dozen pigs trotted gleefully through a green meadow. The whistling winds embraced them under a sunless sky. A bunch of robins cooed from a treetop nearby, filling the air with their cheerful chatter.

At the edge of the meadow, the oldest pig stopped and oinked. 'Oink! Folks, look what's on the other side of this gushing stream—so much corn scattered across the grass! Let's take a break and roll in this wishy-washy mud. Then, we'll cross the stream to feast on our yummy spread of corn.'

So, after playing in the mud by the meadow, the oldest pig trotted off to cross the stream. The others followed closely behind.

'Once we are across, let's take a headcount to make sure we're all in and no one is left behind.'

The pigs nodded in unison.

They splashed and wobbled in the cool water. Some were having far too much fun belly-flopping and twirling about. After a while, they decided to get to the other side of the stream.

The oldest pig heaved and sighed as he tiptoed out of the water. His buddy reminded him to take a head count, so the pig began: 'One, two, three, four, five ... eleven?'

His body froze in shock, and his usually curly tail straightened in a jiffy.

'Hang on! Only eleven! We were twelve—like a dozen bananas! Where is the twelfth pig? Did we lose him? Did he drown?' he cried.

One of the pigs looked confused and said, 'Did a fish kidnap the pig? Oh wait—maybe the missing pig got magical powers and just vanished into thin air.'

The pigs, including their worried leader, ran around helter-skelter oinking in panic.

Just then, an old wise sage, who had been watching the whole scene from a distance, burst out laughing.

'You silly, funny piggies!' he guffawed, stroking his white beard. 'You forgot to count yourself, oh big, wise leader!'

The oldest pig's mouth dropped. 'Really? Wait a minute....' He counted again. 'One, two, three, four ... TWELVE!'

'No one is missing! We're all here!'

The happy pigs did a little dance and soon tucked into a hearty corn feast. The leader pig, all cheered up, never forgot to count himself again.

24. THE PEACOCK AND THE FOX

Once, in the thick of the woods, there lived a sly fox named Reynard. One evening, just as night was about to descend and the sky glowed with twilight, Reynard stood in an open field, staring up at the night sky.

He gazed at the patterns the stars made, grouped into clusters across the sky. The air was thick with the scent of pink bougainvillea flowers covering the trees. Though the fox pretended to be lost in thought, mesmerised by the distant stars and half-moon, he watched from the corner of his eye.

A beautiful peacock had waltzed into the field. He spread his shimmering feathers, a magnificent fan of deep blue and bottle green.

Reynard's tail swished as he thought to himself, 'That peacock is the meal of dreams.'

The peacock tilted his head and asked, 'Reynard, what are you doing?'

The fox turned to face him. 'You know, there are a million galaxies in the sky. I'm merely counting the stars.'

'So, how many have you counted so far?' the peacock asked calmly.

Reynard did not expect this question. He paused for a moment and replied, 'Well, beautiful peacock, the stars are as many as the silly folks on Earth.'

The peacock fluffed his feathers and asked gently, 'Are there more stars in the sky or more fools on Earth?'

Reynard smirked. The mischief shone through his eyes. 'Looks like the fools are more ... just by one!'

The peacock's eyebrow shot up. 'Well ... who might that be?' he said.

The fox brought a furry paw to his chest. 'Well, buddy, it's me. I am the fool. Who else?'

The peacock, amused, asked, 'You say you're foolish, Reynard. Really? How so?'

The sly fox now grinned from ear to ear. 'Well ... just look at your dazzling feathers. Instead of losing my mind over the distant stars, I should be counting the gems and stars inked in your plumage!'

The peacock laughed. 'My dear Reynard. Sly and smart as you may be, your foolishness lies elsewhere. You made a big error in assuming your flattery and smooth talk would let you turn me into your next meal!'

Reynard's ears turned hot. He had been caught—and how!

Without another word or any more pearls of false praise, he spun around and ran like the wind.

'Run, you foolish fox, your trick just trapped you!' the peacock called after him, laughing.

25. THE STAG, THE TIGER AND THE HUNGRY CROCODILE

Long ago, in the heart of a dense jungle full of tangled vines and vegetation, there lived a stag named High Horn. He spent his days playing in the mud, lying in the open field and munching on carrots and blades of fresh, dewy grass beneath a peach tree.

One hot afternoon, the handsome stag grew terribly thirsty. He wandered in search of clean water. Soon, he came upon a sparkling, clear stream. Bending down, he drank deeply, quenching his parched throat with the sweet water.

Little did he know—danger was just around the corner.

Hidden behind a thick bush, a fierce, hungry tiger named Long Leap had his golden eyes fixed on the stag. The tiger licked his lips, ready to pounce on his next meal!

But just beneath the surface of the stream, another predator stirred. A massive crocodile named Great Jaw swam silently through the water, his scaly body gliding and sharp eyes glinting. He, too, had spotted the stag and was waiting for the perfect moment to strike.

As High Horn lifted his head from the stream, feeling full and refreshed, he was ready for a nap in the open field under the fiery sun when—whoosh!—Long Leap pounced from the bushes.

But—wait!—he missed!

Long Leap, with all his grand plans of landing on the stag, crashed straight into the jaws of Great Jaw, who had risen

from the water in perfect timing. Before the tiger could release himself from the grip of the terrifying animal, Great Jaw opened his vast mouth and—

BITE! SNAP!

With one hard bite, he dragged Long Leap into the murky waters.

High Horn froze. His heart thudded in his chest. His eyes grew wide with fear. Moments ago, two predators had been hunting him—and now, he stood unhurt, untouched. He was safe in his beloved forest, free to once again live and play as he liked.

He looked up at the sky. Closing his dark doe-shaped eyes, he whispered a quiet thanks to the universe. 'We, the small, innocent, and gentle, can survive—even thrive—and disappear into the forest when the greedy and wicked predators hurt each other.'

ABOUT THE AUTHOR

Chesta Wadhwani is a journalist and writer passionate about telling stories that connect nature and the human condition.

A graduate of the MFA program at Sarah Lawrence College, New York, she has written extensively for leading national publications. She is also the co-author of *HUM—When Women Lead,* a coffee table book published by UN Women India.

Animal Stories from India is her first solo book, born of her enduring love for the natural world and the stories it inspires.